To Dad, who loved a good word row, born 4-24-24.
And to Hannah, my tot, born in 2002 —M. S.

For Bob and Sōs —A. M.

Text © 2006 by Mark Shulman.
Illustrations © 2006 by Adam McCauley.

Book design by Cynthia Wigginton.
Typeset in Ashwood, Gatlin, Matchwood, No. 13 Type,
and Whitecross by Walden Font Co.;
Rosewood by Adobe; and Iceberg by Adam McCauley.
The illustrations in this book were rendered in mixed media.
Manufactured in China.

Library of Congress Cataloging-in-Publication Data available.

Distributed in Canada by Raincoast Books
9050 Shaughnessy Street, Vancouver, British Columbia V6P 6E5

10 9 8 7 6 5 4 3 2 1

Chronicle Books LLC
85 Second Street, San Francisco, California 94105

www.chroniclekids.com

MOM

AND

DAD

ARE

PALINDROMES

A DILEMMA FOR WORDS...AND BACKWARDS

By MARK SHULMAN

Illustrated by ADAM McCAULEY

chronicle books·san francisco

My name is

That might not sound like a problem to you.

But yesterday it almost **DID** me in.

My teacher, **MISS SIM**,
told us about palindromes.

She said:

> Palindromes are words
> that are spelled *exactly*
> the same way, forward . . .

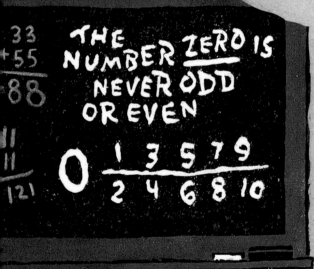

THE
NUMBER ZERO IS
NEVER ODD
OR EVEN

33
+55
=88

0 1 3 5 7 9
2 4 6 8 10

121

AHA!

WHAT A GIG!

TUT, TUT

. . . and backward!
Phrases and sentences can be palindromes, too.

Then she just about
ruined my life.

"We even have a palindrome
right here in class.
Can anyone find him?"

"BOB"

My face became **REDDER** and **REDDER**.

That was just the beginning. Soon it was clear that there were palindromes everywhere.

My **KAYAK**.

AMENI CINEMA

NOW ON:
SPACE CAPS
PARTY BOOBYTRAP
MAD AT ADAM

My **RACE CAR**.

STEP ON
NO PETS

OTTO, my **PUP**.

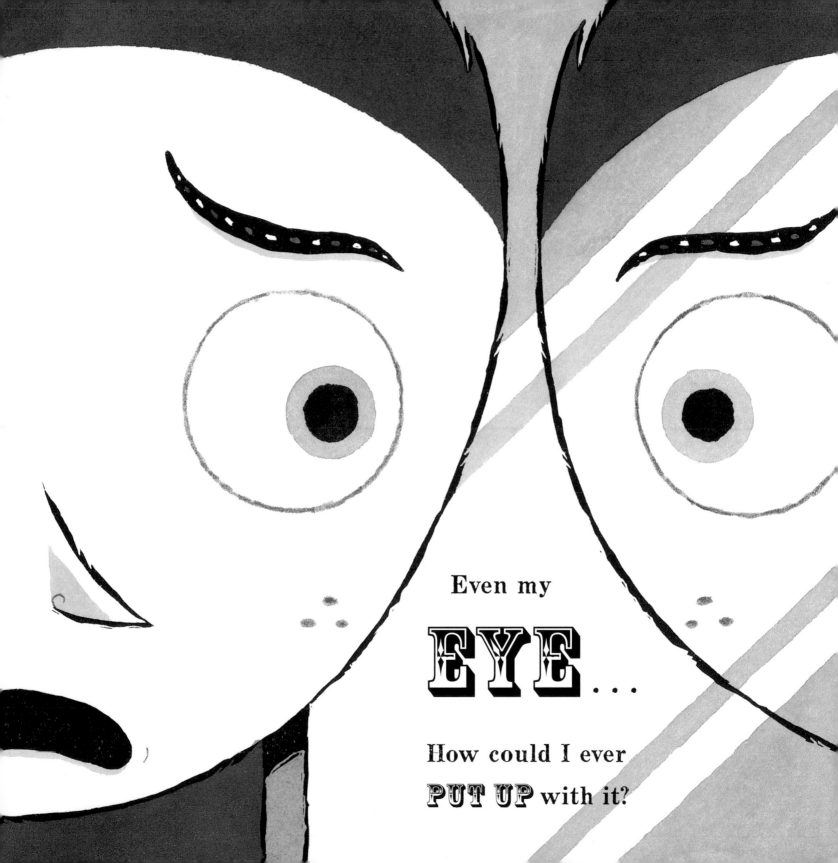

Even my

EYE...

How could I ever
PUT UP with it?

My whole world was going

backward . . .

MADAM, I'M ADAM

MADAM, I'M ADAM

SOLOS
ESTAURANT

DAO ROAD

YELL ALLEY

ELITE TILE
CO. INC.

21J12

. . . and forward!

It was awful.
I needed to tell Mom and Dad and . . . *O NO!*

MOM and DAD

are palindromes!

I ran at **DEEP SPEED** to warn my sister!

I was breathless with fear.

"**MOM** and **DAD** are palindromes!"

I whispered.

MUM

is the word.

DOOFY FOOD

MOM TREBOR

DAD TREBOR

Danger, I **SAW, WAS** everywhere. "You're all palindromes!" I yelled. "Even **NAN**! Our little **SIS**! She's just a **TOT**! In a **BIB**! In a **BIRCH CRIB**!"

OO! GOO GOO!

DOOFY FOOD

SNACK CANS

ANNA gave me that sister look. "**LEVEL, BOB, LEVEL**," she said calmly. "You're being a **KOOK**!"

"Maybe a nut," I said,
backing away slowly.

"Maybe a loony. Maybe
even a big fat cuckoo.

But not a

KOOK!"

The clock struck **NOON**. I knew that would happen. Some kids would take the hint. **DID I? I DID.**

I drank some

POP for PEP.

It made me GAG.

I **DID** a good **DEED** for a **NUN**.
It was a **DUD**.

I tried to run away on a ship.
They had three jobs.

 Run the **RADAR**.

 Fix the **ROTOR**.

 Or **PULL UP** the anchor.

I left without a PEEP.

Suddenly, a brilliant idea exploded like **TNT**.

"WOW"

Palindromes are really just words and there's more than one way to say any word!

ANNA is really Annabelle! NAN is Nancy! MOM is Mother and DAD is Father and I am Robert! It will get better, WON'T IT NOW?

I've solved the palindrome puzzle. From now on,
I'll only use my full name!